RIDE A PURPLE PELICAN

RIDE A PURPLE PELICAN

Rhymes by
Jack Prelutsky

Pictures by
Garth Williams

Greenwillow Books
New York

The art work was prepared as full-color paintings combined with separate black line
illustrations. The typefaces used are Zapf International Light and Medium.

Library of Congress Cataloging in Publication Data
Prelutsky, Jack.   Ride a purple pelican.
Summary: A collection of short nonsense verses and nursery rhymes.
1. Children's poetry, American.   [1. American poetry.   2. Nonsense verses.
3. Nursery rhymes]   I. Williams, Garth, ill.   II. Title.
PS3566.R36R5 1985   811'.54   84-6024   ISBN 0-688-04031-4

FOR GWYNNE, WITH THANKS
—J. P.

TO DILYS, WITH LOVE
—G. W.

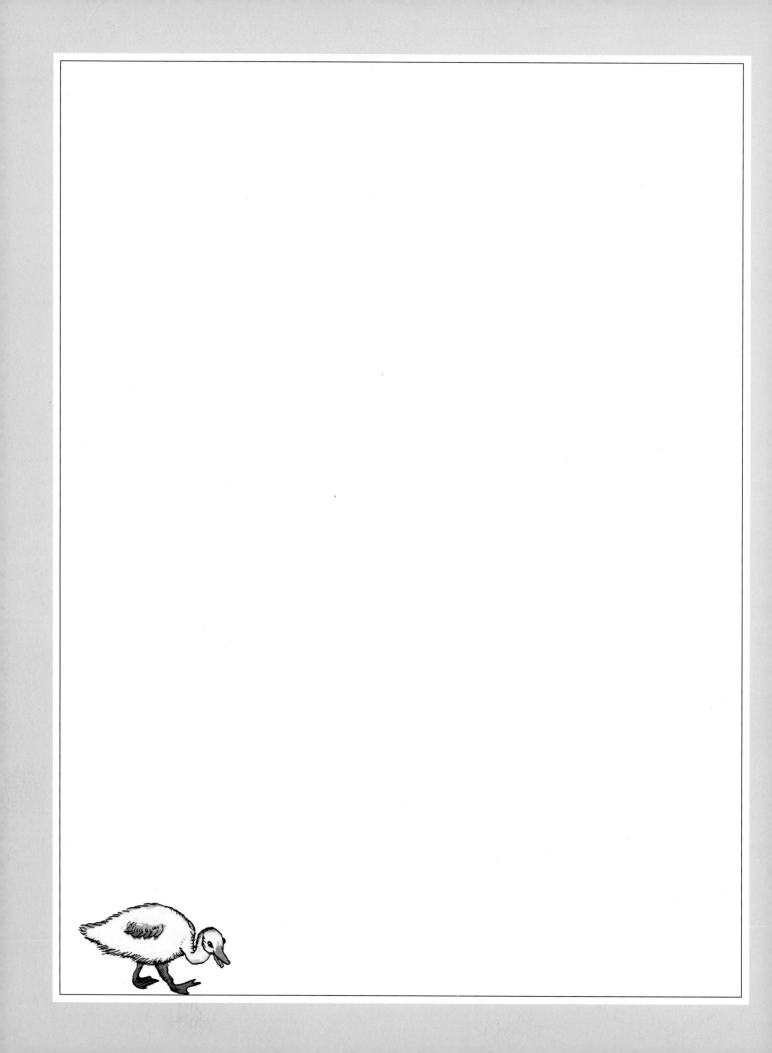

CONTENTS

Justin Austin • 8

Rumpitty Tumpitty • 10

Late One Night • 13

Rudy Rode a Unicorn • 14

Poor Potatoes • 16

Two Robins • 18

Johnny Had a Black Horse • 20

Molly Day • 22

Little Pink Pig • 24

Grandfather Gander • 26

Oh Pennington Poe • 28

Naughty Little Brown Mouse • 30

Timmy Tatt • 32

Parrot with a Pomegranate • 34

Grandma Bear • 36

Jilliky Jolliky • 38

Early One Morning • 40

A White Cloud • 42

Bullfrogs • 44

One Day in Oklahoma • 46

Timble Tamble Turkey • 48

Betty Ate a Butternut • 50

I'm a Yellow-bill Duck • 52

I Went to Wyoming • 54

Cincinnati Patty • 56

Hinnikin Minnikin • 58

Kitty Caught a Caterpillar • 60

Ride a Purple Pelican • 62

Justin Austin
skipped to Boston
dressed in dusty jeans,
he sipped a drop
of ginger pop
and ate a pot of beans.

Rumpitty Tumpitty Rumpitty Tum,
Buntington Bunny is beating the drum,
he doesn't look up and he doesn't look down,
all through the Rumpitty Tumpitty town.

He twitches his nose as he tramps through
    the street,
stamping his Rumpitty Tumpitty feet,
Rumpitty Tumpitty Rumpitty Tum,
Buntington Bunny is beating the drum.

Late one night in Kalamazoo,
the baboons had a barbecue,
the kudus flew a green balloon,
the poodles yodeled to the moon.

A monkey strummed a blue guitar,
a donkey caught a falling star,
a camel danced with a kangaroo,
late one night in Kalamazoo.

Rudy rode a unicorn,
its mane was silver spun,
and west from Nova Scotia
they raced before the sun.

They soared above Toronto,
then north from Winnipeg,
they swooped into the Yukon
and found a golden egg.

Poor potatoes underground
never get to look around,
do not have a chance to see
butterfly or bumblebee.

Poor potatoes never look
at the fishes in the brook,
never see the sunny skies—
what a waste of all those eyes!

Two robins from Charlotte
set out on a stream,
they rowed to Savannah
for peaches and cream,
the peaches were sweet,
so those two little birds
remained in Savannah
for seconds and thirds.

Johnny had a black horse,
Jenny had a gray,
and west from Colorado
they rode one summer day.

They rode to California
to see the giant trees,
then galloped to the rocky coast
to feel the ocean breeze.

21

When Molly Day wears yellow clothes,
finches flutter by her toes,
when she's in her bright blue gown,
peacocks trail her through the town.

When Molly Day is dressed in red,
hummingbirds surround her head,
but when she wears her suit of gray,
no one follows Molly Day.

Little pink pig in Arkansas,
danced a jig with his mother-in-law,
she wore silk and he wore straw,
little pink pig in Arkansas.

Grandfather Gander flew over the land,
he flew to Rhode Island and sat in the sand,
a goose and her goslings sat down by his side,
and they all sailed away on the afternoon tide.

Oh Pennington Poe,
your auto won't go,
your truck is so rusty
it's stuck in the snow,
your horses are sleeping,
your donkey is slow,
and that's why you're weeping,
poor Pennington Poe.

Naughty little brown mouse,
whiskers on his face,
stowed aboard a rocket
bound for outer space,
they lifted off from Houston
on Tuesday afternoon,
the mouse ate cheese that Sunday
in the mountains of the moon.

Timmy Tatt, Timmy Tatt
wore a watermelon hat
as he waltzed in the meadow
with an avocado cat,
but they stumbled on a shadow
and they tumbled with a splat,
and that was the finish
of the watermelon hat.

Parrot with a pomegranate,
pigeon with a peach,
flew to Honolulu
to dance upon the beach,
they danced a pair of polkas,
they danced a polonaise,
then ended with a hula,
and slept for seven days.

Grandma Bear from Delaware
rocked in a rickety rocking chair,
socks on her feet and a ribbon in her hair,
Grandma Bear from Delaware.

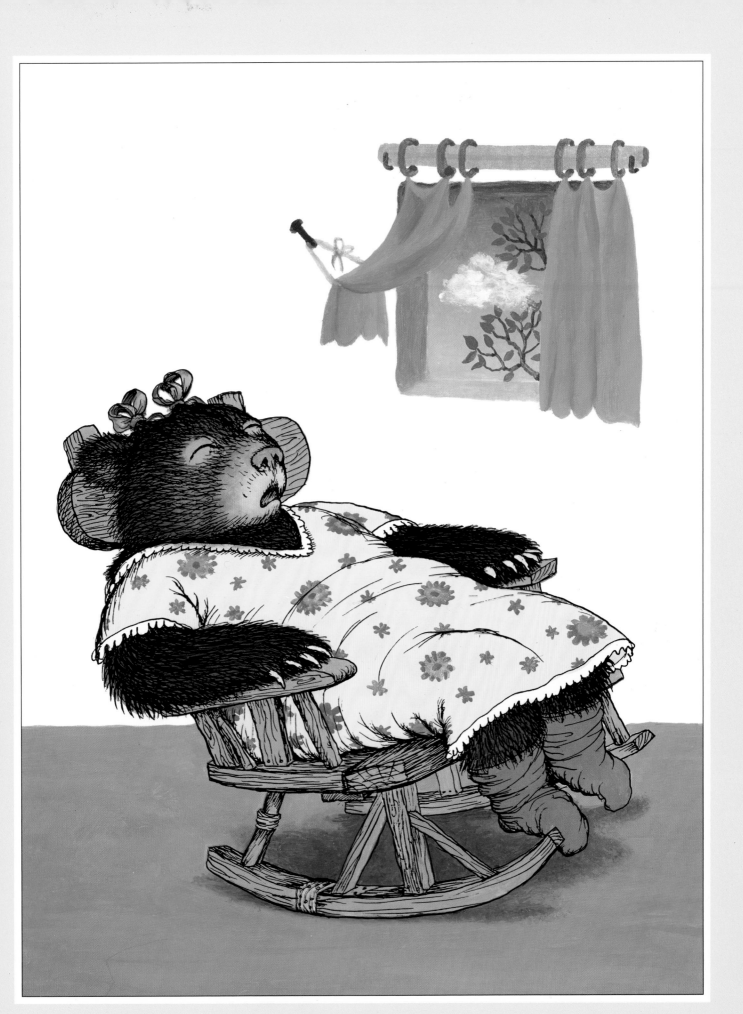

Jilliky Jolliky Jelliky Jee,
three little cooks in a coconut tree,
one cooked a peanut and one cooked a pea,
one brewed a thimble of cinnamon tea,
then they sat down to a dinner for three,
Jilliky Jolliky Jelliky Jee.

Early one morning on Featherbed Lane,
I saw a white horse with a strawberry mane,
I jumped on his back just as fast as I could,
and we galloped away to the green willow wood.

We galloped all morning with never a stop,
where mockingbirds whistle and ladybugs hop,
we drank from a stream where the water
     runs free,
and we slept in the shade of a green willow tree.

A white cloud floated like a swan,
high above Saskatchewan,
the cloud turned gray at ten past noon,
it rained all day in Saskatoon.

Bullfrogs, bullfrogs on parade,
dressed in gold and green brocade,
scarlet buttons on their suits,
fringes on their bumbershoots.

See them tip their satin hats
as they bounce like acrobats,
hear them croak a serenade,
bullfrogs, bullfrogs on parade.

One day in Oklahoma
on a dusty country road,
I heard a handsome ermine
serenade a rosy toad,
I saw a hungry rabbit
munch on lettuce à la mode,
one day in Oklahoma
on a dusty country road.

Timble Tamble Turkey
lived in Santa Fe,
went to Albuquerque
to see the fishes play,
the fishes were in Phoenix
for they had run away,
so Timble Tamble Turkey
went back to Santa Fe.

Betty ate a butternut,
Betty ate a bean,
Betty rode a bicycle
from Exeter to Keene.

Betty rode to Brattleboro
eating carrot cake,
then pedaled on to Burlington
and swam across the lake.

I'm a yellow-bill duck
with a black feather back,
I waddle waddle waddle,
and I quack quack quack!

I dabble for my dinner
with a swish swish swish,
and I gobble gobble gobble
all I wish wish wish!

I went to Wyoming one day in the spring
to hear a rhinoceros trying to sing,
the sound was so strange that it gave
   me a fright,
and I ran to Nebraska the very same night.

Cincinnati Patty,
smaller than a thumb,
rode a mouse to Cleveland
to feast upon a plum,
she feasted for a minute,
and that was her mistake,
for Cincinnati Patty
got a giant belly ache.

Hinnikin Minnikin,
Minnie and Moe,
went to Chicago
to see the wind blow.

The wind was so cold
and the wind was so strong,
it spun them around
and it pushed them along.

It lifted them up
and it swept them away,
they landed in Kansas
the following day.

Kitty caught a caterpillar,
Kitty caught a snail,
Kitty caught a turtle
by its tiny turtle tail,
Kitty caught a cricket
with a sticky bit of thread,
she tried to catch a bumblebee,
the bee caught her instead.

Ride a purple pelican,
ride a silver stork,
ride them from Seattle
to the city of New York,
soar above the buildings,
bobble like a cork,
ride a purple pelican,
ride a silver stork.

JACK PRELUTSKY's poems are bellowed, repeated, and laughed over wherever there are school-age children. *The New Kid on the Block* received many awards and commendations and was an ALA Notable Book. Among his other popular books are such favorites as *The Sheriff of Rottenshot*, *Nightmares*, *My Parents Think I'm Sleeping*, and his many beloved holiday Read-alone books.

GARTH WILLIAMS needs no introduction to book lovers. His classic illustrations for the *Little House* books, *Stuart Little*, *Charlotte's Web*, *Bedtime for Frances*, and *The Cricket in Times Square* are cherished by readers of all ages. His own picture book, *The Rabbit's Wedding*, has been in print for more than twenty-five years. He divides his time between Santa Fe and Mexico.